Who's my Stalker

" FAITH OVER FEAR"
IS WHAT STRENGTHENS ME.

D. G

Foreword

Have you ever been in a situation that you can't really have answers to? Have you ever been scared that someone out there knows all about you – even the things you do in your own apartment – but still can't place a finger on who really the person is? It isn't a pleasant feeling indeed. I don't know if you know about that, but I am sure several people have once gone through similar ordeals. I hear it's not easy at all, and I concur with people that say this because for me, it was a difficult guessing game. One moment you think you know who is behind it all, the next you are all confused, doing a back and forth between separate suspects. Nevertheless, I lived to see another day and can write about my story for you to see just how much I was troubled by this whole issue.

I named my book Who's My Stalker because I want readers to give me closure. I need this closure because, sometimes, it feels like I don't know who to think is behind what I have been going through. Right from the beginning of this ordeal, I understood that someone might be out to cause trouble in my life – or their intentions were good, I don't know. But in the end, I know that I got nothing good out of it. And as I still seek after closure, I feel the gap in my heart – it yearns to be filled so that the rest of my mind and body can rest and focus on other important things of life.

Let's face it, stalking is unwelcome and, in all ways, violates the victim. I feel violated and rightly need closure. In psychology, they say that males that are being stalked could lose confidence in themselves, I keep wondering if the same could happen to me. Perhaps a plethora of questions that sometimes rain down the mind, of course without answers, is a major catalyst to the confidence issue they talk about.

Nevertheless, I had people in my life, and you will see the names as the story goes. In fact, I still have them, in a hard way, and I am sure you know why by now. When everything was going on, I was sure Lynn was the whispering voice. Because everything started taking place after I did not acknowledge her at the bar. Then it got to the point I was thinking there's no way she could be doing this alone. I was contacted 24/7, night and day for months. So I began to think Lynn got in touch with every female I had ever talked to and they began to gang up on me. At that point, I began to think every female was out to get me.

Carrying these feelings around is nothing but a pain on the back. Imagine feeling like tons of people have your number in their phones with just one intention – to keep on sending you messages that had nothing to do with your current standing with them? Worse off, I could not tell who exactly had my numbers – all I could wait for was the moment when the next phone call arrived. It just got things really nasty for me – so who's next to contact me? What are they going to demand from me? Are they going to keep on calling or are they going to up the ante on me and start doing all sorts of crazy things?

I know, these are a lot of questions to be asking in one's head. But for a person in my shoes, it had to be that way because I just didn't know what to expect next. All I could think of was them – and exactly who could that be? Of course, there were some people, or some names I kept on suspecting in my mind. That was all I could do – only suspect them without coming to some sort of solid conclusion. In the end, it really didn't matter what I thought about them, or their role in my current predicament.

In my relationship with Angela, I hated being questioned. So when questioned that was my exit and Angela eventually started to realize this. If you notice in my writing, things happened to the extent where I clearly thought she was responsible. I felt she acted out as such because that was her only way to voice what she has seen. Torn pictures with marks in the face and two single numbers switched around in my phone. I didn't realize until I started writing this book that those were clues.

Nevertheless, I also stated that she was not the only one I suspected of all these things. As such, I could think that Lynn and these other females were out to break up my relationship. I started staying home and stopped talking to girls only because I refused to let them win. When I did that, I was no longer contacted by the whispering voice. A year later, I thought I was in the clear, but that was all a mistake! Many things started to happen all over again, and that is how I came up with these several episodes, once again, narrating how things were going down on many occasions. They literally turned my life upside down, and caused so much pain to me, and even to people that were close to me. I know that it hurts to see people you care about going through all sorts of problems. Well, it happened like that for my friends that cared for me. I never knew that things that happen in your life could affect your inner circle like this until it happened to me.

After those episodes is when I started staying home and no longer talked to girls. So, after that year passed and as soon as I messed up, more letters were attached to our front door to where ONLY Angela would find them. 😒 I began to think Angela had a bright idea because she knew how spooked the whispering voice had caused me to stay home and no longer cheat on her. So I began to think that she took over to keep me from cheating on her. Eventually, I began to question Angela if she was the whispering voice. She would swear up and down that she was not. The only thing that allowed me to believe her was because, if she was the whispering voice, she knew everything that I did on her and she just stayed.

However, in the midst of looking for answers, I found myself treading on the same ground over and over when all I wished to have was good progress so that I nipped it in the bud and got this over with. The only problem was that I was basically dealing with someone that had done their homework and knew exactly what they were doing! The nagging question was, who could that person be?

Contents

FOREWORD

INTRODUCTION 1

INTRODUCING TATE – 10

A BACKGROUND INTO THE STORY 10

THE HUNT FOR TATE BEGINS 35

STAGE 1 48

STAGE 2 74

FINAL CHAPTER..82

Introduction

Everybody has history, and I got mine too. With that being said, I wouldn't say that I must be judged, nor do I deserve to have someone following my every move in a way that scared the hell out of me. The same way I won't be blamed for my past is the same way I wouldn't do that to someone else. I just needed to get that out of the way so that I give you no reason to doubt me – or that I help un-cloud your judgement when it comes to inputting your opinion about who my stalker was.

Basically, I am an organized individual, therefore, I like to express myself from the beginning of the story to what transpired in the end. In fact, I am that kind of a guy that can even give you a nice background to the story so that you understand everything you are reading about. It can only be fair enough for my readers.

Therefore, I want people to voice their opinions about who my stalker was with the full background of the story, including how everything builds up to the unfortunate situation I eventually found myself in. That's why I started with my first relationship, Milla. I know, there is just this thing about first relationships – they are sweet and innocent, yet we grow into something else the moment we start to grow in love with this person. Sometimes you find that the graph that

1

measures your love is growing in opposite directions. She could be growing in affection for you every day, yet for no reason, yours would be growing downward like that of economic growth during a recession!

As a man, I would be quick to agree to this, but that does not mean that every man grows out of it and ends up messing things up, sometimes it's the lady that's found on the wrong end of things, or, sometimes nothing just goes wrong. I wish it was like that for me. It could have avoided all the nightmares that I am going through now. Perhaps it would have been easy to figure out who my stalker was. But just as I have learned about life, it pays nothing to regret. What's done is done!

Therefore, what can we say? Its life, and it's not easy to stay satisfied with just one person, yet it's the right things we should all be doing – so I think.

My second relationship was with Jennifer. While being involved with her, I met someone in college and we had a good thing going on for some time until it ended. Her name was Shawna. With her, something happened, and I don't know how she feels about it right now, but my guess is that she is doing well in her life even when we parted ways in a very unpleasant fashion. I got her pregnant while in college, and with many things in the balance, I felt I wasn't ready to be a dad, so I convince her to have an abortion. I know, right? You could ask questions, why was I the one to suggest the abortion to her? Well, sometimes we make decisions that are not too familiar with people, but, as long as they seem to be the best option for everyone in the picture, my guess is we should go for them. I did it here and Shawna, at the time, understood things from my point of view. In the end, we had an agreement that made things a little easier for both of us.

Nevertheless, the relationship with Shawna ended, mainly because of the abortion. I wouldn't get into the details, but it ended and we both had to move on. I am just glad that we managed to put it past us what had happened with the terminated pregnancy. Well, when we date people, we know them intimately and from all of them, you can have a certain opinion, be it wrong or correct.

I then met Angela, whom we have been together since the first day of our love. She now is the mother of my children! I know that I called it a 'list' but it's merely because of how I put it down here. I think I still am one of the guys with the fewest past relationships, and naturally, that should have allowed me not to live a life where someone from my past was stalking me. If the list was very long, perhaps we could have said there was a high possibility of having been with someone with bad habits.

Nevertheless, for some time, it just wasn't about my past relationships. I also questioned my group of friends. You know, these things happen, especially when you feel like you're being cornered with nothing else to do or no one else to look up to for help. I just needed someone to blame. I needed an answer because in a way, answers bring solace to a troubled heart. Sometimes you just believe in things even if you know that they aren't true. I know, many of you can attest to this — you could believe in half-truths, or unfounded allegations so that you end up giving yourself some false hope. I guess I was at that point in this whole mess. But deep down, I truthfully do not believe it was them. I don't believe so because they worked as hard as I did to make sure that I bring this whole thing behind me. I hated this sometimes, but they were always there to give me a huge shoulder to lean on!

These were the guys that were always by my side. We did many things together. And if I say so, some people would be tempted to think that we were up to regular mischief that guys could get involved in, but not with us. Of course, we could count a few things that were not the kind you could be proud of, but we were good most of the time. My friends and I played basketball at parks all the time and went to the clubs on a regular basis. We loved the vibe on the basketball courts in the parks. You know, when life seems so simple and everybody can sort of come together and connect. Yes, that is what exactly used to happen with us back in the day.

Regarding clubs, it was also one of our regular activities. I am sure it even sounds better now to sweat a good part of the day on the basketball court only to go and relax, or enjoy ourselves in the club. We loved the music and the vibe that everyone else in there used to bring. I can't say I am much of a dancer, but when music played, I couldn't help but also shake my body.

Speaking of the people in my circles, I mentioned already that I suspected that Lynn was the stalker because mainly the fact that she acted in a way that was completely surprising. She had spilled something to the wrong person. And you know how it is, it only takes a few words to the wrong person to cause complete chaos in another person's life. That is exactly what she did to me.

Lynn was a coworker of Angela's sister's boyfriend which she didn't hesitate to make him aware that she was a friend. Imagine that kind of information getting to Angela? That was completely uncool of her to do that.

So I had to ask her why? Because of that conversation between her and I, I began suspecting that she could be the one stalking me. At least she had revealed that she had some ulterior motives, especially after making someone close to my life aware that we were friends when that was not the correct version of things.

Nevertheless, I guess I should say that Angela's character, for me, was great. Despite the many things that I did, she showed me that she could be a patient individual that cares about building something more than fulfilling our egos – just like how many of us would do it. I tell you, with the kind of things that used to happen – and still happening in my life, it could be too much to handle. I don't know how many people won't be pushed to the limit by such things.

So, Angela - she was in her senior year of college and was very popular and so determined to finish school. I know, many people are eager to finish school, but there are a few others who would succumb to small pressures of life – good or bad – and end up failing to finish school. So, it's because of this that I had to highlight how much Angela was determined to complete her studies because she never fell to any pressure, whatsoever! Nevertheless, no matter how good someone can be, if they are constantly pushed to the brim, they could explode to many people's surprise. It's just how it is, and as for Angela, we will see how she held up during the many roads I took her down for a trip – sometimes bad, and sometimes good ones.

Speaking of people's characters, there was Tate (you will know about him later in the book). The man was a manipulator and womanizing person. He was so selfish, and the one thing that struck me the most about his attributes is how he was so determined to get any girl that he wanted. He never took no for an answer and knew how to make every girl say yes to his shenanigans. Even if the girls knew that he was bad news, I was surprised to see them fall for him, head over heels! Who's this guy?

Nevertheless, we were born differently, and that's OK. During the stalking period, I was so confused that I lost trust in everyone. I thought I was going crazy. Everyone that was in my circles became a prime suspect. It was just one of those confusing moments in my life. So, the period where I suspected everyone only came to an end when my confusion turned into fear – the fear of having someone eventually placing a dagger in my back as I prepared to take a bed in my home. You can only imagine the fear! But I am grateful that I am still alive to tell the story.

So, I haven't mentioned my friends yet, but I had those really close to me – you know, when you have friends there are others that you just talk to, and there are others whom you call your 'inner circle.' Well, my inner circle is composed of James, Jamien, Kenneth and DeSantos. I love these guys and call them my little partners in crime, not that we were into crime, but because we used to do things together – as family would do! These guys always had my back. They were there for me even during the times when my own family couldn't be there for me.

I was certain that Lynn was the stalker. It was like that for some time until a time when my focus was shifted to someone else. Sometimes you think that some things must not be done, or thought about, but situations always put us in a corner that is difficult to pull ourselves out of and we find ourselves pointing fingers to where they are not even supposed to be raised toward. So, some things that took place led me to question Angela. During that time, she became my prime suspect and I was sure that she was the one stalking me. You know that time when you're so wrong about something but somehow, you just find yourself believing the contrary! I was like that when I suspected Angela.

You could be asking how I then became so sure that she wasn't the one stalking me. Well, besides the fact that she is nicer, EVERY TIME that I questioned Angela something dramatic happened. More so, she did something that really showed me that she wasn't the one - she put it on both her parents' graves that she was not the stalker. And some of the things that used to happen led me away from her. Let me just say that all the odds were being taken away from her. For example, the fact that the stalker once slashed all four tires on our only vehicle, making it harder on us, just showed me that she wouldn't do that also to her. She disowned some of her good friends. My kids' lives were also threatened – of which she is the mother. Therefore, all these events that were taking place could only lead me back to focus on Lynn.

Forgive my paranoia, it's just that there were so many things that were happening to me during that time. I had to do something - I had to find the person behind this so that I could claim my life back. You can imagine - my stalkers called my work phone all night long, every night, it just goes to show the depth of their hatred against me. They would ask all sorts of questions, for example, why I cheat and for me to leave Angela. They were telling me that Angela was dumb for staying and calling her all sorts of names, some of which I really thought were derogatory. When I wasn't at work, they would call my cell phone and it would ring all the time. I would think of switching it off, but then think that there are some other people in my life who will need to contact me. You can imagine, it was just a dilemma that I was in. I never received a phone call while Angela was around. When they called, they only whispered because they didn't want me to know their voices. Perhaps the fact that Angela was never around to witness the phone calls led me to suspect her of being behind it all.

As for Angela, they only contacted her using letters. No phone calls. Anything I did they knew about. And they notified Angela by placing letters explaining everything I did on our front door only for her to find. It was as if they knew exactly when to place them so that she would be the only one to find them. This whole thing was just messing up with me. While looking at all this, I could only think that the stalkers were always watching my house. How could their timing be so perfect? How could they time it so perfectly that it was only Angela who received the letters? And how could they time it so perfect that when Angela was around, I would receive no phone calls?

Even when I was confused about this whole thing, I knew one thing for sure – I knew that whoever was stalking me, 'she' had help from other people. It was, however, scary not to know how many people were up against me.

Introducing Tate –

A Background into the story

I spoke about how much I like to give a full background to every story that I tell, and I stay true to my word. Here, I give the background to how I got to this point of writing a book inspired by events that no one would like to live. So here it goes!

In this chapter, I am going to talk about myself like it's someone else because I want to read and really get a deeper understanding of the person that is me! Sometimes, it feels good to sort of step outside your body and watch yourself doing things, no matter how bad they look. As for me, writing about myself like this gives me that opportunity to have that glimpse into myself!

A soft spoken young man from a small town gravitates to the football field hoping his athletic ability, in years' time, would lead him to a rich future. Although temporarily distracted by the presence of temptation from girls, Tate's mind was focused on the importance of making it to the NFL. Some may have assumed he was scared of the presence of a girl, but their concerns were the least of his worries.

Chances of him getting someone pregnant or catching an STD were a chance he refused to take.

This kind of determination is what you see in many young people in High School that aspire to become pro football players. Tate was more like that and wanted to make a name for himself. With the summer break entered in his senior year of high school, he was introduced to a girl by the name Milla. She had this presence he could not resist. She left him stunned by her beauty. A few hours later on the phone, Milla became a distraction. Tate chose not to avoid losing the love of this stunning young lady for football. With him falling in love, his passion for the game slowly started to fade.

Friends were seeing the sudden change occurring as Tate and Milla's bond grew stronger. A teammate of Tate's by the name Jacob tried to intervene by questioning his loyalty. "You mean to tell me you are never going to cheat on Milla with another girl?" This guy said it as if cheating was something normal – even something that every guy, including Tate, was expected to do. For Tate, it was easy to reply no when everything about Milla was perfect. Weeks before graduation, there was only room for one true love. The love for football was no match for perfection. Young and naïve, corrupted by love, Tate was blinded, with no worries as long as Milla was by his side.

Love blinded both these two, and before they knew it, they agreed to move away from their homes so that they could 'enjoy' each other without the noise of boring parents. However, they say that life is the greatest teacher of humans, and they're so right when they say that. Tate and Milla soon realized that becoming independent wasn't as easy as they assumed. They searched the whole area to find a place of their own, but unfortunately, they found that they were not in a place that they could afford the cost of living on their own.

Therefore, they both had to move back home with their parents. Shortly thereafter, Tate and his friend, Daniel, got an apartment together in Mumphord, TX. The distance between Tate and Milla became a problem, especially along with their sexual interaction. The feelings that he once had for Milla when they first met started to fade. The flame had dimmed and his mind started to wander as his eyes began to seek. Even though the flame had weakened he was so deeply in love with Milla the bond he had with her could not be broken. As months flew by, the more Tate's attraction for other girls began to build. He was having a very difficult time fighting these thoughts. There was no way around them. His mind got to the point where it was full of thoughts.

He found himself questioning these thoughts. "Is this it?" "Is Milla going to be the only one?" For Tate, finding himself having conversions with other girls had him feeling guilty. So, he had to do what's right and broke it off with Milla. He did this not to hurt her because it was in her best interest and he did not want to be unfaithful to her. He thought too much of her to ever betray her like that. Tate, soon after the breakup with Milla, found himself single and available for other girls. He started to date other girls.

A year or so later Tate realized that he could have possibly made a mistake by letting Milla go. Dating all those other girls just wasn't all that he thought it would be. As a result, he reached out to Milla hoping they could try again, but unfortunately, she was involved with another guy and had moved on. Tate's heart was empty but he had no choice than to move on with his life. He found himself becoming home sick and moved back home with his parents where he came across a high school friend. With her, it was enough to start having a female friend that he could connect with.

Tate's intentions were not to get heavily involved with Jennifer, but one thing led to another and there he was in his second relationship. This relationship was different. Nothing like the first. It was somewhat like a blur. During this relationship at the age of 20, Tate left his parents' house to attend school at Kilgore Junior College. Now surrounded by a new environment, he became selfish considering the relationship he had back home. Tate ran into another old high school friend, a couple of days after arriving, who also attended Kilgore Junior College.

Shawna and Tate had competed against each other for 4 high school years. They were both well-known athletes when it came to sports. Tate and Shawna found themselves hanging out with each other a bit too much than needed to be, which led them to becoming very close. This was a problem because Shawna was in a relationship of her own. Tate's first time cheating didn't feel so good. He felt guilt. Then one afternoon Tate noticed he had several voice messages on his answering machine from Shawna telling him she needed to talk to him, and that it was very important. He got in touch with her and she told him that she has been feeling very sick and has been throwing up all morning.

At this point they were in panic mode. Before jumping to conclusions, he and Shawna get a pregnancy test, and it came back positive. "What do we do now?". Being that he and Shawna were both involved in separate relationships, they only had one option. Tate and Shawna decided on having an abortion. Things were never the same after that. Shawna became very unforgiving toward Tate as if he influenced her to have the abortion. Things got so bad that Tate dropped out of college and moved in with an old high school classmate who lived in Doomes, TX.

Eventually, he moved his girlfriend Jennifer up to Doomes to live with him. It sounded good at first, but at the time, Tate didn't know what he wanted. There were days he wanted to be with Jennifer, but for the most part, it was as if he just didn't want to be alone. I know, it sounds as if he was using her for companionship, but it was like that, and that one of the things I didn't like about Tate – he was so selfish to the extent of using the nicest people for his own selfish gains.

The relationship he shared with Jennifer was dreadful. Tate regretted it sometimes, but continued to try to make it work because he didn't want to just give up on another relationship. During Tate's relationship with Jennifer, he was messing around with other girls. The more he was messing around with these girls, the less he became guilty of his cheating. As a child, Tate found out that he had four other siblings whom he did not know about. At the time, he was confused by this because he thought he had known all his siblings. Not only did Tate's father cheat on his mother, but his father was also involved in two other relationships in two separate towns all along with his mother being in the dark.

The pain that Tate's mother endured due to his father's infidelity hurt Tate too. Even though he was a young boy, his love for his mother caused him to feel the pain that she was going through. It was on that day that Tate made a promise to himself that he refused to be anything like his father and he would never cheat on his significant other like his father did. Little did he know that it was a promise he would not keep. Even though many men are found wanting on this end, it doesn't take away how noble it is for a man not to cheat on his significant other.

Sometimes Tate would use the excuse that she was the one that pushed him to cheat. But in reality, it was just something that he chose to do. Jennifer and Tate left Doomes, TX and moved to Kingstown, TX. Two weeks living in Kingstown, Tate was already bored out of his mind with no friends. Tired of being cooped up in the apartment with Jennifer, he decided that he was going to go see what Kingstown had to offer. While driving around, he was listening to the radio and heard how Club Extreme is the place to be. For sure, this was the place he was also going to try out sooner or later.

As such, he ended up at this place where he was surrounded by very attractive girls. But because this was something new for him, Tate found himself feeling lost and clueless. For anyone observing, it was clear that he wasn't from around. Soon, he was approached by a girl introducing herself to him, which led to a night of shared conversation and drinks. The night led them to spending time at her place. One thing led to another and the next thing he knew; it was 5 o'clock in the morning. Jumping up in panic, he told the girl that he has to go. Already knowing that he must come up with a story, he would have to explain to Jennifer why he was getting in so late. Luckily for him, when he got home, Jennifer was in a deep sleep.

Tate was becoming more of a mischievous person than he used to be. He now would come up with these crazy ideas that would only lead to trouble. On the night he slept over at this girl's house, he decided to take her panties home because he figured it would be cool to start a collection. This 'bright' idea of his would soon lead to regret and nothing more.

Before Tate got home, he hid the panties in the inner pocket of the jacket he was wearing that night. For him, it was brilliant because Jennifer would not be able to notice – or so he thought. But to his surprise, he woke up in the afternoon to Jennifer staring at him directly in his eyes while holding these panties in her hands. At this point, Tate is so annoyed with Jennifer that he really didn't care. There was really no way to explain why he had this girl's panties. So he decided to flip the script and attack Jennifer by letting her know that she was wrong to be going through his jacket.

At this point Tate couldn't care less about what happens next. So he asked, "So what do you want to do?" Jennifer, being highly upset and bothered by Tate's treatment, said she wants to be taken to her parents' because she was done with this relationship. Tate was happy to comply because, in his mind, all those beautiful girls from the club were waiting to be exploited. Minutes into this quiet, awkward drive, Jennifer turned to Tate and said, "So you're not going to even try to convince me to stay?" Tate, without looking back at her, said, "No, if you want to go home, I'm going to take you there." Jennifer replied, "I don't want to go home, I want to be with you."

As soon as she said that, Tate turned the car around and headed back to Kingstown. Why Tate continued with this relationship knowing he had doubt was unclear. It was like he needed a way out and Jennifer was not allowing him to have it so easy. She must have been madly in love with him even though he was too busy with the other girls to notice it. I guess the arrogance was growing in him by each day!

But I guess wishes always come true, no matter how bad they look. Tate needed a way out and this one day provided an opportunity to do so. He needed to make a phone call, so he headed downstairs of his and Jennifer's apartment to make the phone call at a nearby payphone that was in his apartment section. The phone was occupied by the time he got there. There was this guy using it, so he walked around his apartment complex in search of another. He found one that was free and took his phone call. By the time he was done with the conversation and hanging up the phone, the other guy that was on the other payphone was coincidentally walking by, catching Tate's attention.

Seeing him again, he thought he should just break the ice, so Tate asked him about playing basketball just to strike up a conversation. I'm new to the area and I'm bored out of my mind. Well, my name is Jamien, we play here from time to time. In a desperate bid of finding new friends, Tate proceeded to tell Jamien how he would like to go out to some clubs. In response, Jamien said that he has family and friends coming into town this weekend and they will be going to a few clubs and he was more than welcome to join. The sound of that was music to his ears. Finally, he would have more reasons to get out of the site of Jennifer to his newly found friends.

After meeting Jamien, one thing led to the other, and he found his circles growing, so much to his delight! Now Tate was being introduced to the club scene and spring break just so happened to be right around the corner. He was invited to go to South Padre Island for the first time. Tate was getting introduced to this all at once and he got really excited. But there was one problem – Jennifer was still in the picture. He was still hopeful that their love would be their prior levels, but sometimes we hope for the things that we know would never work – all because we want it to work so badly.

Months have passed since Tate met his new friends and things definitely have changed. At this point in Tate's relationship with Jennifer, he was even more unsatisfied emotionally and sexually, which was leading to the end of their relationship. It was slowly eating into their romance and only a matter of time before nothing more was left. Perhaps Tate's new friends and lifestyle had something to do with it, but it was probably overdue, simply put. Maybe the problem was with Tate because this same occurrence happened with Tate's first girlfriend, Milla. It appears that after about 2 years of being with one person, his sex drive with them just fizzles out, he does not desire them the way he did in the beginning. Instead of finding a way to fix this, he never really cared because he had no much regard for his girls feelings – it was only about HIM and how he felt in his body, or what he wanted to do for himself.

Nevertheless, Tate had a very hard time being sexually satisfied. It was very difficult at times causing him to have to think of other girls while having sex with Milla. He was very ashamed of this. Milla would say occasionally while having sex with Tate, "Why are you taking so long? Are you not attracted to me?" There is nothing worse than hearing that question from the person you loved. Tate would deny it, but the truth was that sexual feelings that were there in the beginning, were no longer there. Being the guy that Tate was, he wouldn't allow himself to hurt Milla by telling her the truth and have her think she was the problem so, of course, he lied.

It was around the 2-year mark and at this point, his sexual attraction to Jennifer was gone. Tate was finally ready to end his relationship with Jennifer because, in his opinion, it was a complete waste of his time. When he tried breaking up with her, things didn't go as planned. Jennifer would not accept the fact that the breakup was what Tate really wanted, so she made it very difficult for him and made excuses of why she could not leave. Jennifer, trying to hang on to the relationship with Tate, caused conflict to where eventually her parents had to be brought into the picture. Her parents were finally able to convince her to leave and helped her get a place of her own.

At the age of 22 Tate is now single again, but this time, he told himself that he would not jump back into another relationship for a while. He just wanted time for himself and to experience life. For some reason, friends of Tate's would use the phrase "wet behind the ears" when describing him. At first, he didn't understand what it meant. When explained to him that it meant immature or lacking experience. Tate thought differently. They would make these comments because they felt as if he wasn't aggressive enough when it came to the girls. They considered him to be scared and shy. There were many times Tate could remember his friends telling him, "You're a good looking guy, you should be up front trying to talk to these girls rather than hiding in the back."

Tate was always given a hard time because of his shyness. So he started believing the saying that he was wet behind the ears was true. But that was soon to change. Before Tate knew it he had a new group of friends that he would hang out with every weekend. Hanging out on Thursday, Friday and Saturday became the new norm for Tate and his friends. Tate started hanging out with his new friends so much that eventually, they all ended up becoming best of friends. For the most part, his experience with the club scene was always exciting. Tate loved meeting new girls. I mean, he really loved the girls! He became so confident in himself that talking to girls became so easy, it all became somewhat of a game.

In Tate's eyes, he was a different type of guy. In his eyes he did not feel as if he was a player, but felt he was more of a ladies' man. He believed that, as long as he didn't lie or play any games with the ladies, then how could he be characterized as a player? Whenever Tate would meet girls, his first response would be, "I just recently got out of a relationship and I need time for me, but I would love to get to know you." Making sure the girls understood clearly what he was saying. He would say to them, "If you and I happen to be in the same club, don't be afraid to talk to other guys because I will not be upset with you. However, I would expect you to allow the same when it comes to me," just to be sure they had that understanding.

Everything was almost perfect for Tate. But, from time to time, he would have that one girl who would try to test him. This was something he would not tolerate and he would dismiss them immediately. Tate would not allow any girl to disrespect his wishes. Some would disrespect him and then come back acting as though nothing had happened; however, he wasn't having that. If you disrespected him once, he wanted nothing else to do with you. Unfortunately, those who attempted to approach him after they had disrespected him, would soon find out the hard way that they made a grand mistake by approaching him.

That was one mistake they would never make again. Eventually, Tate had been with so many girls that there were times he would find himself forgetting some of the girls he had already been involved with. One night while standing in the club with his friends, he saw a girl from afar. He leaned in close to his friends and said, "That's a nice looking girl right there". Tate was always on the lookout, trying to find the best looking girl in the club.

As soon as she got closer to him, he leaned closer to her and whispered in her ear, "How are you doing?" She responded with an upset tone in her voice, "Why haven't you called me!". Tate was now confused by her response because he had no idea who she was. But in his mind he knew that she could be one of his past girls and he had just lost her 'face' because he had been with many of them, and was never serious with any of the girls.

So he allowed her to talk because as she was speaking, he was listening to her every word to allow himself time to remember who she really was. There were times when Tate would be bored with himself, so he would ask his friends to pick out a girl for him and his task was to get her. Believe it or not, half of these girls Tate would not even call after getting their phone numbers. He just liked doing it, to see if he could. When it came to relationships with any of them, for some reason after having sex with them once, he would become uninterested in having sex with them again. Tate even had a verse of a song that reminded him of himself that was written by Jay-Z called Excuse Me Miss. Every time this song would play in the club while him and his friends were together, they would look over at him and laugh. The verse was, "Everybody's like, He's no item! Please don't like him. He don't wife 'em, he one night 'em!"

Tate was so stuck on that verse that he even had it set as his screensaver on his laptop. Some of Tate's friends would laugh at him because they would say things like, "What have you been doing to these girls?" Like he was doing some extra sexual pleasures with them. Tate would laugh and make jokes about it. His reply would be, "You know the saying... Once you go black, you never go back? Well, once you go Tate, it's too late to change things around." Even when he grew up always hearing how men and women would talk about how great sex could make a person fall in love, Tate had a hard time believing that. Well, especially after all the girls he had been with and for that to be true, he would have thought by now he would be in love.

For the most part, Tate felt as if he was sexually satisfied with the performance of the girls he has been with. So, in his mind, the saying about great sex can cause a person to fall in love was definitely out of question. The single life for Tate fell short once again. But this time, it was very unexpected because at this time in his life, any type of serious relationship was out of the question. Entering Club Extreme with a couple of friends during a wet bikini dance contest had Tate's eyes caught in a deep stare. The way she moves her body up on stage had him intrigued.

The competition ended and she was announced as the winner, sending her into full excitement as the crowd went wild. Tate was on the search to find this girl that he was so intrigued by. He was searching through the crowd with her nowhere in sight. Then there she was, at the center of the dance floor! He made his way to her with no hesitation and softly grabbed her by the hand and asked her name. The conversation started rather quickly as they began to dance. Then out of nowhere, their dance was interrupted by this girl with a rush of excitement! This girl said, "I told you I was going to win, three times in a row. At that moment, Tate realized that he had made a mistake. Disappointed with the situation because he knew this was a task he would not be able to complete. Figuring there was no way around the situation, Tate continued to show interest in the girl he assumed was the girl on stage.

As the night passed and it became closer to the end of the night, Tate said to the girl, "Well, can I get your phone number? She hesitated and said to him, "Well I don't know if I should, because you seem like you are a player." This is a word that Tate despised the most, despite behaving like he was one. He hated being described as a player. So he said to the girl, "What makes you assume that I am a player?" She replied, "Because you have that pretty boy look about yourself."

"So just because I look this way, you assume I'm a player?" He responded while obviously being annoyed by her remarks. He continued to convince the girl otherwise, along with proceeding to ask her for her phone number. He could tell she was holding back from giving it to him but at the same time, her actions revealed that she wanted to, but had to continue to make it difficult. By this time, Tate was becoming very impatient. So he said to her, "I'm going to ask you one more time for your number. Can I have your number?" She hesitated once again. And, without hesitation, Tate turned away and walked off, leaving her standing there.

Even when he walked off, he did not really get disappointed because now he was back on the mission to find the girl. Once again, he found himself searching for this girl. Closing time was coming around quick, which meant he had to work fast on finding her. Tate heard the DJ announce the last song of the night and shortly after, the lights would be switched on as security escorts people out of the club. As he was exiting the club after the song had been played, there she was crossing the street and approaching the area which everyone was exiting! He quickly had to think fast on how to get her attention. So he said, "Excuse me, I don't know if that was your friend or whomever, but she's something else."

Before he could even get out what he was about to say concerning the girl, she said to him, "That's my sister." (As if things couldn't get any worse.) Tate, feeling a little down at the moment, responded, "I know you may not believe me, but truthfully, I introduced myself to the wrong girl." She appeared to be slightly confused by this. So he said, "Let me explain, I entered this club and spotted you on stage in the wet bikini contest. From that point on, I was searching all over the club to find you. I spotted this girl which I thought was you, only to find out I was wrong. How I figured that out was because your actions on stage were the same as when you approached your sister and I, while we were on the dance floor. By that time, I knew I had approached the wrong girl. Being that you had seen that I was with her. I knew that there was no chance of me getting to know you. So I continued on trying to get to know your sister."

That was quite a long explanation, but it was enough to get a response from her. "I understand, it happens often. People mistake me and my sister for one another." Tate told her, "Your sister assumed I was a player by the way that I look and gave me false hope which caused me to become uninterested. Which I didn't mind because the girl I was looking for is standing before me now." She laughed and said, "Whatever." Tate always believed if you can get the girl to laugh the better are your chances in getting to know her. So he said, "Well my name is Tate, by the way. What's your name if you don't mind me asking?" "Angela, she replied.

"So, I see you won the wet bikini contest". He responded with his heart pumping, seeing that the conversation was still ongoing. "Yeah, I've won every time I've entered and I do it only for the money," she said. He said to her, "There's nothing wrong with that." Tate had a way of getting girls to do things for him in a way that would have a person thinking he was only using them. He said to Angela, "So how about you take me out to eat?" Angela was surprised, "What? You're supposed to take me out to eat." They laughed together before Tate said something more, "You're the one who just won free money in a contest. You can take me out to eat. Please... I'd like that."

Angela laughed and casually responded, "Okay, but not tonight because my friends are waiting on me. That's where I was headed now to find them." So they exchanged numbers and she walked off to meet her friends. During the exchange of the numbers, Tate noticed his friend, Daniel, trying to get his attention to come over to where he was and standing next to him was Angela's sister. Waving off to his friend "no", Daniel approached Tate, telling him Angela's sister wants to talk to him. But he explained to Daniel he is no longer interested. Walking back to the car and crossing their path at that moment was Angela, and Tate walked her to her car. Tate was so intrigued by Angela that all his attention was focused on her. He made her laugh the entire walk to her car. Once they approached her car before opening her door, Tate turned her towards him and began to sing. "I can't believe it's real. I can't believe it's true. I can't believe its happening. I can't believe it's you and I can't believe that you are here with me and I am here with you."

After singing, he had really taken her off guard, so it became easy to casually kiss her goodnight – which he did. Oh how Tate loved impressing the girls with his singing, and it hardly failed! As soon as Tate got in the car, Daniel handed him a piece of paper with Angela's sister's number on it. He immediately got upset with Daniel because he felt as if he was being put in a bad situation since he was already focused on Angela and didn't want her thinking he had anything to do with getting her sister's number. But at the same time, Tate was wondering why Angela's sister would give him her number now after seeing he was now talking to her sister? He was now thinking to himself that it was very odd for her to now want to give him her number.

Nevertheless, the day was over and ushered in a new one. For Tate, it was a great day because that's when Angela came by for a visit. During the visit, he wanted to take her outside and enjoy nature with her. "It's nice outside, so how about we take a walk and maybe that will give us a little time to get to know each other?" They came across a small diner, nothing real fancy, just a little area where they could sit down and relax. They found themselves spending all afternoon together – something that Tate rarely does when it comes to girls, but there was something different about Angela. Later that evening, they ended up at Tate's apartment and they decided to watch a movie.

Everything was going perfect for Tate as was expected. He had a way with the girls, and for some reason, they felt very comfortable with him. Just another name about to be added to the list, Tate thought to himself. The way she moved her body and undressed herself brought chills to his skin. Her touch was like a touch he had never felt before. Definitely, it was a night that was about to change his life. The next day, he was very anxious about telling his best friends about the girl he had met. The following weekend, she blessed him with her presence once again. A week later, it was as if they were inseparable, to where somehow she ended up staying more frequently at his apartment until she eventually moved in completely.

Tate had no interest in hanging out nor going out with his friends anymore because he found himself wanting to spend all of his time with Angela. A month into seeing Angela, he asked her to stop taking her birth control because he wanted her to have his baby. Things were definitely moving extremely fast, causing Tate to do things that he normally would not do. Tate knew from the beginning that he was highly attracted to Angela, sexually, which caused him to act in such a way. A couple of weeks after asking Angela to stop taking her birth control, she discovered that she was pregnant with his soon to be first child. You would think, by Tate's actions in everything that was going on with Angela, which things were going great.

But a few months into their relationship, he began to miss hanging out with his best friends and it was just a matter of time that his selfishness would get the best of him once again. Tate's intentions of going out with his friends were innocent in the beginning, but it was just a matter of time that the temptation would get the best of him. This would be even more of a task for Tate. How does one juggle having a pregnant girlfriend at home while interacting with other girls without getting caught? Tate's had a way with his girlfriends that some might not understand.

After his first couple of relationships, he started to convince himself that any girl he became serious with would fall deeply for him.

Why his girlfriends would become so emotionally attached towards him was indescribable. Some might say he used it to his advantage. Taking advantage of these situations caused an uncontrollable emotional hurt that his girlfriend's chose to endure, but he never felt the need for anyone in a relationship to be controlled. You may call it manipulation because, for every action he took, there was always a reason behind it – things definitely always set to fall in his favor.

It would appear that Tate was everything that a girl could ask for. He was very protective and dominant when needed to be, and blessed with good looks, great sense of humor, romantic, loving, sensitive and very caring. A blessing that he took full advantage of, not thinking of all the pain it would cause. From the looks of things, you would think Angela was just the girl Tate wanted in his life. She was very athletic and very much into sport as Tate was himself. She was also in her senior year of college which was a major attraction for Tate.

Angela was a very strong determined individual. Every word she spoke expressed how important it was for her to graduate and be successful in life. Now expecting her first child, you would think she would be less determined, but that was far from the case. She pushed herself even harder. 9 months later at the age of 23, Tate had his first new born baby girl. Their first child was definitely a blessing for the both of them. They were filled with excitement, enough to fill a whole room! But the new adventures as parents were soon to come – which is not always that easy.

Angela's caring for their new born along with having to continue with her schooling was very difficult. Tate's behavior changed temporarily due to the birth of his baby girl, but in no time, he was back to his selfish ways. Angela clearly suspected his actions but feared the thought of losing him so she kept quiet. She was stuck in the middle – does she address Tate's actions and take the chance of him abandoning her or is she better off saying nothing?

Just a few weeks after the birth of their new born, Angela approached Tate in tears. At that moment, he was worried that Angela had found out something concerning him and other girls and it had him uneasy. With hard tears falling down Angela's face, she cried out to Tate, I'm pregnant and I can't do this! Tate embraced Angela with full affection, letting her know that she is not alone, that she has his full support and told her everything is going to be okay. You would think that this would cause Tate to step back and care less about the thought of trying to get with other girls, but not even that was enough to keep his full attention. Bad choices can sometimes come back to hurt a person if they're not careful.

Now moving back to Lynn's story, she somehow found her way into Tate's life, and it was during the same time as Tate was with Angela. After finding out that Lynn was a coworker of Angela's sister's boyfriend, Tate continued to interact with her. While constantly reminding himself of this bad situation, he was building trust for Lynn, and he became too comfortable in the process, which he would soon regret. Although Lynn knew that Tate had a pregnant girlfriend and child at home, she continued to pursue his attention. Now Lynn was also aware that Angela's sister's boyfriend works with her, and therefore, it was just a matter of time before he knew it. But she wanted it to be like that – she was determined to find a way to let it be known that she was a friend of Tate's.

One evening, Angela said to Tate, "Hey, a friend of yours works with my sister's boyfriend." While being told, Tate was playing it off as if he was uncertain of whom she could be referring to as he shrugged his shoulders. He did not say anything as he tried to avoid a bad situation with Angela. Angela continued to question this friend with concern. "Well, this friend tells my sister that you and her are really good friends."

No longer able to avoid what is being brought to his attention, he saw that he now had no choice but to intervene so that he could clarify the whole situation. "Oh yes, Lynn, her and I have been friends for quite some time now." He said while mentioning that he was unaware that Lynn was a coworker of her sister's boyfriend while trying to convince Angela that this friend was of no importance. Angela knew her limits when it came to Tate, so said nothing more. Tate patiently waited to call Lynn to address this situation in private. He waited until he arrived at work later that night. The right approach was very important to him because he knew that the wrong approach could become very threatening towards his relationship. Picking up the phone while nervous because he did not know how her reaction would be like, he dialed her number.

Lynn answered the phone and there was laughter and loud music playing in the background. "Hello." She spoke into the phone in a loud voice that was seemingly fighting its way through all the noise in the background. "Hey, can you talk?" Tate wanted the chat between them to be civil and matured so that nothing goes wrong. But it seemed as if Lynn was busy being concerned more about whatever was happening in the background, and that riled Tate.

Tate realized that there was no way he was going to get Lynn's full attention, so he asked her, as calmly as possible, why she had to say something about the two of them to someone knowing him to be Angela's sister's boyfriend? Then it was as if everything went quiet. An unexpected reaction of pure rage came from Lynn that the only response that Tate could get out was to hang up the phone. He went back to his night expecting a text, or a call shortly after, but his phone stayed silent. Days went by and it eventually became weeks. Still, there was no sign of Lynn. Assuming he was in the clear of what could have been a very bad decision was a major relief.

Months later, while standing at the bar ordering drinks and being acquainted by the presence of a soft touch, Tate was stunned by the reappearance of Lynn as if nothing had ever happened and everything had been forgotten. He showed no remorse as if she did not exist and continued on with the orders of his drinks. Lynn stood at a distance with hopes that their presence would gravitate, but nonetheless, she was highly mistaken. It appeared that Tate could never be satisfied with just one girl. Why company himself with other girls when he has everything he could ever ask for was a question he had for himself after every encounter.

At the age of 24, Tate was blessed with a newly born baby girl, a 10-month-old baby girl and the mother of his children that adored him faithfully.

She questioned his behavior given the many good things he had going on, yet it seemed like it wasn't enough for him. Questioning Tate's actions in the past lead to pain and regret. His response to questioning his actions was something of pure ugliness. He felt if he was being questioned, the one doing so already knew the answer to the question. So why not tell you what you did not want to hear.

Overtime, after interacting with other girls, Tate started noticing things out of the ordinary – things happening that led him to believe that Angela was doing things subtly to make him aware of his actions. Giving his time to other girls led to unexpected occurrences. Hiding pictures of a girl that Tate placed in the backpack that he carried with him to work every night.

Arriving to work and viewing the photos, he found something very disturbing. The photos were slightly torn down the center and circles from a marker were in the girl's face. Unable to contain his anger because of what he was seeing, he picked up the phone and made a phone call to Angela. His voice tone was harsh. "Why are you going through my backpack?"

The Hunt For Tate Begins

So, yes, that was me living my life up there. I accompanied myself with girls like it was no man's business, I did not feel a thing for them. Angela lived with me, as you have read, but I still had little respect for her when it came to cheating. Instead of me taking a more apologetic way of talking to her after discovering that I no longer had full privacy with my photos, I went all mad at her. I still don't know if that was a good idea. Nevertheless, as I shouted at her after discovering that someone knows about my photos in the backpack, I was in the dark about the things that were to come. I am sure you are reading and calling me all sorts of names for not being able to anticipate what then befell me in the coming months of my life.

But who could have anticipated such a thing? I mean, it's one thing to hide things from your girl, and it's another thing to suspect that someone is about to start stalking you.

Going back to the day I saw that my lovely photos had been tampered with, Angela was confused as she responded to me over the phone. According to her, she knew nothing about them and who would have tampered with them. In fact, she went on and blamed our daughter for that. But how could a one-year-old know how to circle the face of a girl in a photo? That, for me, was utter nonsense! I just couldn't understand how our daughter could have managed to do that. More so,

35

the fact that the photos were tampered with and then placed back in the bag made me suspect Angela more while disregarding her reasoning that it could have been our daughter's fault that I now had marked photos in my bag.

"By the way, why do you have photos of another girl in your bag?" Angela's question just came from out of the blue and caught me unaware. "Damn, she's so good!" I said in my heart while the rage was still going on. I bet she could feel myself breathing over the phone. But as usual, I was never going to satisfy her with panic or another half-baked response. My voice had to show her that I am still the man in her life.

"So why wouldn't she just talk to me rather than going over my stuff and putting weird marks on them?" I was assuming that she already knew what was in my bag, but instead of talking to me first, she decided to take matters into her own hands. However, I think about these things and now understand her reasoning. I mean, I was never the type of a person that my girl would sit down and sort of 'talk' to me about my issues. That would have just made things worse. So, if she was scared of talking to me about my issues, I really understand her for doing that.

This kind of attitude helped me get past many tricky situations with my girls. It was gold for me. At first, it's something I would do on purpose, not meaning it to hurt anyone, but just some slick move I would use to get myself in the 'safe zone', but as time passed, I discovered that I started doing it out of rage. And the rage was because

I felt that I was always right and therefore deserved to be treated as a saint. See the irony! I was never a saint in all my dealings with my girls. I know, this contributed so much to what I ended up suffering, but still, no one deserves the kind of stuff I went through as someone tried their best to send a message, or rather get their revenge on my past mistakes.

Nevertheless, I was mad at Angela for my photos, but that was just the beginning of the whole story.

I went through a lot of pain because I was in the habit of quickly getting fed-up with a relationship. If there is one thing I have observed in life, when women commit, they do so with all their love and they want something fruitful – even something they can rely on going into the future. But for me, I was always in it for very short periods of time. What makes matters worse is the kind of charm I would use to get them over the top. They would, therefore, fully fall for me because of all the nice things I promise them on the first day. But a couple of sexual encounters later all that promised passion would be slowly waning. I hate to even think about that, but it happened and here I am!

Sometimes I would sit down and ask myself, how does one show full attraction when meeting someone for the first time and then days later, get absolutely no interest from that person? I couldn't understand for the life of me how someone could lose interest in me days later with no warning of exit, so I picked up the phone and started dialing numbers of those I had affairs with in search of an explanation. Contacting these girls as if they were personal projects needing to ease my mind.

37

Nevertheless, I still needed answers and I had the nerve to pick up the phone to call one of my exes because I wanted to find 'closure'. Absurd as it sounds, I needed to do that because it had gotten to the point where it was starting to eat me up. Eventually, I became more certain that something extreme was definitely taking place. It wasn't just something I was doing out of utter mischief, there had to be something wrong in this whole equation.

As I continued to make these calls, when they did, I would pause, take a deep breath as if I just lost focus and suddenly forgot why I was making these calls in the first place. But the truth is that I feared that the answer I may receive would be adverse. You know, for someone as arrogant as I am, I am always scared of getting a response that wouldn't suit my agenda. I always want to have things my way even if I am not the one in charge. So as I called them, I still expected to get the kind of responses I wanted. I was so scared of getting something contrary to that, but it was very much possible.

It was unusual to be calling girls and ask if anyone had called them and asked about me. So, as I asked the girls if anyone had called and asked about me, the response was the same, "No." It became like an old record playing in my ears as I moved from one girl that picked up my phone call to the next. On that day, I realized I had done something seriously wrong. Or, I could have reminded someone how bad I was to them, and they started cooking up a plan to get their revenge against me. It was after making these calls that the stalking started to intensify. At first, I could not describe it as stalking because I had nothing like that in mind, so I thought they were just pranks pursued by someone who knows me. So I waited for the day they would reveal themselves to me and we both laughed about it, but it never came. So I decided to write about it.

Nevertheless, I found strength to ignore all these 'pranks' and decided to live my life in full. I went away from home, and I felt like I was free to do whatever I wanted. Freedom was something I really loved. It is the reason why I used to be arrogant and not want any girl to tell me what to do — because I always wanted to be free. So here, while away from home, I had every reason to explore my freedom and use it anyhow I wanted. There was no eye staring in my direction, and that meant enormous freedom to do whatever I wanted while ignoring those calls and so forth.

I grew to become a 'social maniac' if there's anything like that. Socializing with numerous girls came natural for me, especially given such an environment of huge temptation. I had no worries of having to explain my current relationships because the distance made me untouchable, so I thought. But you know, the world is big enough to hide your shenanigans until someone who knows you, spots you in a compromising position. It happened to me and I had no idea when it did. That's when I discovered that it really is a small world we live in.

I was surprised to receive a phone call from Angela about a phone call she received concerning some of my nightly interactions with another girl. According to Angela, these interactions felt threatening as her informant had described it to her. For her to ask me like that, she must have been told how bad the situation looked because like I said, I wasn't the easy type to approach, especially where accusations were involved. So she must have been so sure of what she wanted to ask me before making that phone call. So, by just getting that kind of a call from her, I discovered that I was in for some real explaining to do.

I was shocked and could not hide it from my face. It really sold me off as a clear sign of guilt decorated all of it. I discovered that I had to change the narrative quickly. I was frustrated that how could I let someone spot me in another city? I had thought that it was impossible for something like that to happen, but it ended up happening and now I had some explaining to do. At this moment, I could only play back some of the nights when I was away in my head to try and see if I, indeed, had come across a familiar face. If I could remember, that person was going to be in for some rude awakening for snooping their nose in my business.

As I did that, I needed something to keep Angela distracted, so I kept on questioning her about the person who brought this to her attention. I kept on telling her that I had no idea who that person was. I wanted to explain myself out of this even though I knew that the situation with her having no proof or evidence of my entanglements with another woman meant that there could be no conviction. So with all the noises I was making, it was just for keeping my ego intact – that I don't allow her to think that she was right by entertaining accusations brought in by a third party.

After a few days, I found myself looking down at an unexpected caller wondering why someone would be calling me using a private caller ID. I was hesitant to answer as I softly said hello. There was silence from the caller on the other end. I repeated myself, "Hello." Again, silence from the caller on the other end. Assuming I was called by mistake, I ended the call and went on with what I was doing. But moments later, my phone began to ring once again. Glancing down at it as the screen said, incoming private caller, I did not hesitate to say hello. And once again, I was greeted with silence from the other end of the line. What followed there were questions in my mind as I was momentarily taken from what I was doing.

After the calls from the private number I was still me, still looking for fun. And, as the weekend was approaching, I had to go back to the usual Tate that I was. I, therefore, picked up my phone to make a call to the weekend mistress. But numerous unfruitful attempts of reaching out to her left me with more concerns as to why was there no answer? I wondered and left her alone. This time, it wasn't me that had ignored her, so it was bothering me. I hated being treated like this. It only had to be me doing it to girls and not the other way around.

On the other hand, as weeks went by, the private caller kept on calling me and it began bothering me. Now I knew that this was not a mistake, someone was really out to send a message to me. But why would they call and not say anything? I kept on asking myself with no response. Finally, the caller decided to talk, but it was with an unpleasant

41

emotion that came to me. She sounded like a lady, I could hear it even if she was disguising her voice with a low pitch whisper trying to make it very difficult to hear.

"Can you speak up; I can't hear you." I said as I was eager to hear who was really calling me all these weeks. As I asked, the whisper slightly rose. "If you enjoy the company of other girls so much, why not just leave her?" This time, I could hear the words even though I could not tell the voice's owner. "Who is this?" I could only respond as I felt a knot tying up in my stomach. I could tell that someone was really up to cause some problems, but what was scary was the fact that I did not know what they were up to. I could only make assumptions later.

Whispers became silent as the sound of a dial tone reached my ear. It left me gazing in space as I wondered what may come from this alarming phone call. Deep thoughts of whom this unknown caller could be left me uneasy. I tried to think about it most part of the day but came to no answer. Therefore, I could only point in the direction of my most recent affair. Lynn! Dreading to dial Lynn's number, I gathered enough courage to call it. And when I did, I did it because I felt threatened, hence I had to act. I reached her number, only that this time the voice from a strange lady in my phone told me that the number was no longer in service. That really left me with no doubt about who's behind the whispering voice.

After this, I could only think of the caller's next move. So I anxiously awaited upon the day she attempted to reach out to Angela.

42

This really had me exceptionally intimidated. But days passed with no sign from the unknown caller, and it felt like months. But her silence, even though it left me in the clear of what could have been a rude awakening, had me living on the edge. After some time, the calls started all over again. This time, they could ring my phone and then cut it off before I answered. Sometimes they would just allow me to answer and not say anything even though I could hear the breathing coming from the other side.

I was so annoyed about this and really wanted to get an opportunity to tell the caller a piece of my mind. But how was I going to do that since we did not speak? The caller seemed to have one agenda, which was only to confront me about my affairs and seeking revenge. It appeared to be the sole motive of this whispering voice.

On some days, I would be seated, clenching my jaw and worried about the calls that I had first assumed were just a prank. Afraid to answer because of who's possibly on the other end had me worried. I sometimes watched my phone ring until the ringing tone went silent. Seconds later the sound would come back once again. Answering my phone only to be alarmed by the whispering voice, "Why must you cheat on her?" The voice would ask me.

"Lynn, I know this is you! What do you want?" I sounded so desperate while seeking to put a face to the whispering voice. Still, the voice wouldn't give up the identity of the culprit, but continue to question my behavior, leading to me hanging up once again. Arriving to work the following nights was almost like a repeated series of déjà vu for me. Answering my phone, as the whispering voice spoke of my activities in the night really became a bother.

"I hope you had a good time last night and by the way, we loved the outfit you were wearing." The voice would sometimes brag while sending me into a complete state! It had my head rolling all day. This was becoming real now.

As all this madness continued, I started realizing that there could be more than one person doing this. Now even more confused under the impression there is more than one suspect, frustrations of questioning myself what I could have possibly done to cause things to take such a turn for the worst, causing the unknown caller to seek revenge grew bigger. I could see that these people were now always lurking in the shadows, watching my every move with intentions of ruining my relationship with Angela. Being contacted by an unknown caller caused me to question everything and everyone around me. Consciously making unwanted decisions being controlled by the presence of a voice irked every inch of my soul.

Now I was stuck between protecting myself and putting my family first. Even so, I wouldn't know how these people were going to hurt my family, but I knew that this couldn't be good at all. Most would say this is an easy decision, but selfishness and stubbornness is what got me here in the first place.

But I kept on waiting for the day that the caller would contact Angela. I thought that was going to be their final move to complete whatever game they were playing. Weeks became months as the phone calls became more frequent, but yet Angela still appeared to be unaware. Desperately thinking of ways I could possibly dismiss the unknown caller, I changed my phone number. The move made sure that I was temporarily unbothered until when I arrived at work and my work phone began ringing.

When the phone rang, I was so hesitant to answer because I knew who was on the other end. When I finally gathered the courage to answer, I was greeted by a soft whisper that entered my ear.

"So are you ever going to leave her?" I was tempted to respond but elected to stay silent because I now realized that the sound of frustration and desperation to come out of my voice was exactly the intentions of the whispering voice. Bothered by the sounds of continuous rings throughout the night, I disconnected the receiver to silence the unknown caller. Therefore, I registered a success for the rest of the night since I never had to answer a call from this strange caller that I strongly suspected was Lynn.

But I was very wrong if I ever thought they were going to give up on me. I just did not know that they were going to up the ante on me as time passed. One night, a surprising alarm by the front door caught my attention. Ding dong, ding dong, and looking down at my watch, I was concerned why someone would be randomly pressing the doorbell at my job at an odd hour of the night. Slowly approaching the door, I feared who it could possibly be. I just did not want to think about the response to this question. "Just go and see." I whispered to myself as I continued to tip-toe to the door that suddenly was looking like it's one of those from the haunted house in a movie. But yes, it was still my door – and wasn't a haunted house at all! The stalker really had messed up with my mind!

Right now, in the middle of the fear, I forced myself to remain calm with the possibility of revealing the person behind the whispering voice. Slowly reaching for the door knob with the intent of surprisingly catching the person who's responsible for the private calls, I swung the door open only to be greeted by my own reflection standing in a glass door. I walked further into the driveway then continued into the street. Looking in every direction my eyes could possibly see, I remained in anticipation of this person behind the whispering voice only to find no one but myself standing alone.

Some days later while looking down at my phone, there was an incoming private call. It can't be! I thought to myself before pressing the answer button. "Hello?" I hesitantly spoke into the phone as I kept my ears as alert as those of a wild animal in the jungle. If I had to survive, I really had to be this alert every time I responded to the private calls. It was the only way that I was going to reveal the identity of this troubling person.

"Why not just leave her?" The voice, once again, whispered the same thing that had now become a broken record. Hanging up my phone, I immediately changed my number once again. After several attempts of changing my phone number, I realized there was no escaping the private calls. The worry had now spilled over to Angela. I would step into our bedroom to find Angela with a concerned look on her face. She would be troubled as she hands me a disturbing photo of her that would have been taken from a distance.

This is now happening! With a look of distress from some random guy catching her off guard asking for her name. Feeling threatened by a photo being tossed on the table identifying her as the person he was seeking. Visions of Angela being approached by a stranger riled me, they pushed me to the brink! My jaws began to clinch as my body shook with rage. My mind was, indeed, set to rage, but more so, concerned of the extent to where this was going to end. I felt completely lost in the whole mess. How had things got so out of control?

Stage 1

One day having my boys over for some drinks while standing in the parking lot listening to them discuss their affairs. It was cool for most as they are being reeled into each other's stories being told. Even though they were enjoying themselves, I just couldn't afford the luxury as I had to keep one eye open and an ear out for strange bystanders. I was very sure that somehow Lynn was listening to cause trouble for me, my relationship or even my friends. You know, there were no boundaries when it came to stalkers - all they wanted was to make sure they caused pain and anxiety around me. The most boring thing was that Lynn was so careful in doing this, and no matter how hard I tried, it was just too difficult to catch her in the act. But I remain hopeful that one day the chickens would come home.

I was always feeling this uncomfortable, creepy crawl behind my back. It was such a feeling that someone is surely listening in on all what we were saying, especially when I would be the one talking to my friends. I would, from time to time, glance over their shoulders in search of an unfamiliar face. Sometimes, I would ask my friends to lower their voices in fear of being heard by the unknown person. Knowing what the situation was already like with my life, they would comply and pause and then continue with their conversation after a few moments.

After a while, I would ask them, once again, explaining that someone was listening in on our conversations. It was really an awkward moment. My boys were trying to enjoy themselves and my paranoia was playing a major role in their night as well. But I was too busy being worried to notice any of that. It was just a disaster waiting for the right, or bad moment to explode, depending on which side of the fence you're standing. As for me, it was, indeed, a disaster waiting to explode in my face.

After a while of doing this, I noticed that my boys were getting concerned about my behavior. At this moment I was all over the place and nowhere near any of that "calmness." You know, at that moment, the idea of laughing at the thought of having a stalker wasn't so funny for me. But in time the drinks began to taste smoother as my night became more relaxed. Under the influence when temptation presents itself, crossing their path was a sight to see. Temptation as he and his friends began to stare. Her beauty was something difficult to disconnect. Snapping his friends out of their deep stare he reminds them of his stalker. Under the influence of temptation, lead them to the proceeding of her wanted attention. Like, how could I allow myself to fail to temptation when it's what got me here in the first place.

Later on, some days after our eventful night with the mistress crossing our path, letters were placed on my front door only to be found by Angela. They were addressing everything about me and my friends' nightly encounter, I mean everything!

Every decision that I made was known to these people. When you come to think of it, you would think that the unknown person was my own shadow. With my mind racing all over the place, the thoughts of how someone could be so consistent and correct from a distance caused me to believe that I was losing my mind. Grasping in several areas of my body, I would search for some sort of a chip implant because it was strange that someone would know my exact location at any time. I would be questioning myself if God was personally punishing me for all my past wrongdoings.

In the end, I feared losing my family altogether because all these things were coming directly to Angela. So I decided to remove myself completely from affairs. More so, I distanced myself from society. At this moment, I was at a breaking point that I questioned everything and everyone around me, including my best friends. Whoever was behind this had done the most damage in my life. Removing myself from society felt like I had my life completely stolen from me. At this moment, I could look at myself in the mirror in the bathroom and just think, "I hope you're happy, Lynn, you win! You took it all from me. You took everything and I am just this sorry person living life in hiding." It felt so sad, I even lost some weight but Angela was happy that she got to see more of me because of the ordeal.

Besides getting phone calls, my stalkers had other means to get into my life. They used letters to communicate to Angela. And, as much as the letters were addressed to her, I knew that it was a way of sending a message that we can get to your family and whatever you do, we have means to tell that to her. This, I thought was meant to instill fear in me because the more Angela knew about my dealings with the other girls, the more she would fight with me and that was just dangerous as it could lead to our separation. This was a direct threat to my relationship with the mother of my children. Just like the volume of my own phone calls, the volume of the letters that Angela received from the stalkers kept on increasing.

One morning, I could see myself as the old man stumbling from a pile of letters in his hands. In fact, it was like a classic story about an old man that left his home for a whole month and when he comes back, he goes straight to the mailbox to check for his letters and newspapers that he found in their tens, resting in his letter box, waiting for his return. And, instead of taking them into the house in batches, he decides to just go for it all at once and puts them all in his weak arms almost tripping himself as he walks back into the house.

That was me when I opened my door carrying those letters, all of them, addressed to Angela by the stalker causing havoc in my life. Why were they contacting her alone using letters and not me? If they could get their hands on my number, I was sure they could get Angela's number too? So why choose a different means of communication when it came to her? These were all questions that sounded like nothing more than just rhetoric as my head spun. Carrying all those letters in my hands, dressed scruffy in the morning and with a confused-looking face, I surely could be easily mistaken for a mad man. Would you blame me given all that was going on? Perhaps I was getting mad!

As I entered the house with more of these letters in my hands, stumbling both in my body and mind, I really felt overwhelmed by this whole situation. I could feel the weight on my shoulders and some strength was leaving me. I questioned Angela how she was able to receive these letters without coming in contact with the stalkers? Angela would try to explain the situation the best way she could, but nothing made sense to me. All I could do was keep on guessing who my stalker could be. At this point, Angela and I took a very funny curve – like she never remembered to question me about the other girls because we were now fully focused on the stalker, whoever they were.

It's so funny how a bigger crisis, as you see it, can make you lose focus on another form of a crisis. That was Angela, she forgot about the crisis she had where I would always be with different women, sometimes get caught and deny it all! Even though what was happening was really ugly, it gave birth to something nice between myself and Angela. The first thing was me realizing that she was a strong girl that had supported me through my moments of madness when I went around being involved with all these other girls while she was with me. In addition, she also stood with me even when my past actions were coming back to haunt me.

I felt like thanking her for both forgiving me and carrying my load willingly. But my pride stood in the way, and I only decided that I would thank her by way of staying faithful to her. The truth is that I was now scared of losing my relationship with her. I mean, who wouldn't, seeing that she was this strong young lady that could stand for all the nonsense I put her through? So, in fear of jeopardizing my relationship, I made it very clear to my friends that if any female was seeking my attention, I was not interested. My friends were told (by me) to never bother introducing me to anyone new because I was just at a point where I wanted to spend all my time with the people I should have been caring for the most from the beginning. But I guess I had failed them in many ways since they were now being scared of the stalker together with me. I was supposedly the protector of my family that turned into this huge villain – I hated thinking about this because it came to my mind over and over again, especially when I thought about how my dad had kept children on the side without my mom's knowledge. I hated to think that I had also let down my own family.

When I was with my friends, spending time at the club, I always made sure to hint to them that if any female was asking for me they should say I am not interested. That was me getting serious with my family. I would get to the club, enjoy some time with friends and go back home to my family. I guess the stalker, instead of setting me apart with Angela, had actually helped me become a better man to her. Even though the situation was still very difficult for her. How can one keep on loving a man that is being haunted by ghosts from the past? And the same man can't even tell which ghost was haunting him because they are just too many? As you can see, my life was just so complicated, where would Angela fit in that whole web with many strange women, some I wouldn't even remember?

But when with friends, there is no telling what could end up happening. You know, hanging with friends can sometimes lead you in the wrong direction, even when that's not something they are trying to do. I figured out that when you want to completely change your life, you have to do the difficult thing and just change your lifestyle completely. As for me, trying to change was always going to be difficult because my friends and I loved the girls and the club scene. I wasn't going to fit in if I decided to completely change. It was just a way of life for us.

As predictable as it was, I assumed my friends went against my wishes. This was besides the fact that I had precisely explained to them that I was not talking to any females while we were in the club or anywhere else. But once they mentioned she was a good friend of mine by the name Kris, I found myself being happy to see an old friend. In the end, I spoke to her with no worries of the wandering eye because she was a trusted friend, who just so happened to be in town. Even though I could feel the presence of the stalker staring us down I felt like I just needed to enjoy the moment of a longtime friend. She noticed that I was distracted and tried to calm me down. Indeed, her tricks worked. I found myself momentarily forgetting about the stalkers as I enjoyed an adult conversation with her. We spoke for the better part of the night and honestly, it was so refreshing. Her conversations were so refreshing that I forgot all about stalkers.

As we were about to leave the club, we started planning to meet up with each other the next day for lunch and eventually exchanged phone numbers as we agreed on a place. The club closed and we all left for our places. You could be surprised when I say I left right after the club was closed, well, because that wasn't a part of me – it was my habit to stay in the club until it was closed. I wasn't a person that was shy to be the last one to leave if it went down to that. Fortunately for me, besides my friends, it seemed like a couple of other people in our area loved staying late in the club.

Nevertheless, the next afternoon arrived and I picked up my phone to dial Kris's number so her and I could go grab lunch before she headed back home out of town. Dialing her number, I was surprised just to get an unreachable number. Shocked, I rushed to think that perhaps she was one of the stalkers. Why then did she give me a number that suddenly doesn't work? I tried again and again, and after a few attempts, I still didn't understand how a number could be unavailable after I just talked to her on the phone the night before. Was she now thinking twice about meeting me just after a few minutes' chat in the club? Could she be the stalker? Or did she learn about my recent predicaments from someone else and she chose to not get involved with my messed up life?

In the end, I chose to stay calm and ignore it because I had figured maybe something was wrong on her end. After all, my life needed some calmness without adding to potential drama situations like hanging out with another girl that was not Angela. With me having given up on her, which was unlike me after such a short time, I stayed for an hour and noticed I was receiving an incoming call with no name attached to it. I responded to the call and got surprised to hear Kris asking what had happened to me calling her. I said I was just as shocked as she was, I explained how I had tried to call her to no avail and had many questions running in my mind. But I did not tell her about my paranoia that almost kicked in with the whole drama with the stalker.

Later on after dropping the call, I decided to look into her number and compare it with the one she had called me. Comparing the incoming number to the number I had stored in my contacts, I noticed that two single numbers had been changed around, making it difficult to notice. Once I noticed that, I got angry and went straight to Angela. I questioned her if she had gone through my phone. I must say that Angela had managed to stay with me and all my bad behaviors because she had studied me and knew how best to deal with me. So, if she flipped the numbers in my phone, she did it to protect herself without confronting me because she knew that doing so was just going to make things worse.

So now because I had noticed, we could talk about the subject of another girl that she knew she couldn't just come up to me and ask me about it. More so, if I had asked her about what she would have done with my phone in my absence, she would deny. In the end, I felt, what she wants, she gets and I couldn't be too upset with her if I wasn't for sure if, indeed, it was her doing it without concrete evidence. I enjoyed spending time with my friends and it was part of my daily routines to meet up with one of them. Sometimes we would meet in groups. I guess spending more time home was difficult. Even during the time when I had decided against spending time with the girls, I still did not take most of it and availed it to Angela, my friends got to get the most of me when I should have been home with Angela, enjoying our beautiful kids, but I always had some ideas.

Regarding the stalkers, I was never safe anywhere. They seemed to follow me every time I got out of my house. The feeling really disturbed me, but I got some courage when I realized that they were not out to hurt me because if they did, they could have caused so much damage to the ignorant me. Their aim was simply to destabilize my life. They wanted me to live a miserable lonely life without Angela and my children. It was obvious that whoever was behind this was really bitter and did not care whatever happened to me as long as I lived in pain for the rest of my life.

I honestly felt like I was tired of running, so I could no longer look around and check if anyone was following me. I would just get out of my house and visit my friends randomly. I needed to live my life, especially not knowing when this whole madness would end. So one day when I left the house, I walked across the parking lot to my friend's place. I found him waiting for me because I had called to tell him that I was on my way. When I got inside, I took a seat, kicked off my shoes and slid the recliner back. James was in a relationship of his own, but you know how it is, us young fellas liked to enjoy ourselves from time to time.

Even though he had his problems in his secret "relationships" he managed to control the situation in his own way. You know, it was like my own episodes, only without being threatened by stalkers. No one can say their relationship is perfect and I can speak for my boys, especially when it came to James. Because at the end of the night, pull up your seats because it's about to be a showcase. On this day he appeared to be at peace. They had not been fighting for some time and I'm pretty sure things were going quite smooth in his secret "relationships." It was easy to see that he was super relaxed when I entered his home.

As soon as I took my seat, James was alarmed to hear his phone ring from out of the blue because he was having a nice time and forgot he had put it in his shirt pocket where it made a lot of noise as it rang. I laughed because he really seemed startled by the sound of his own phone. "Hello?" He casually responded not even thinking about the possibility of someone out to get him. As he responded to the call, I realized there was no straight response from the person on the other end. As for James, he sat up straight as he also shifted gingerly on the couch. That really got me worrying right there, and I was right.

As soon as I saw him looking towards me while on the call, I knew that it was them calling his phone. By now, there was no guessing the extent they would go to get phone numbers of the people that were close to me. As I listened in on the conversation, I heard James say, "No, he's not around." But he looked scared. I knew it was them asking about me. He was about to hang up when he took the phone back to his ear and then rose quickly to give me the phone as I watched in silence. I was still surprised by the sudden change of mind as he gave me the phone.

"Why not leave her? It seems you love other people more than her. Why keep her?" The whispering voice said and just hung up on me. I gave the phone back, surprised that now they're calling my friends' phones too. Stuck in silence we're both shocked about this recent event.

"Why would you give me the phone? You should have stuck to saying that I wasn't around." Bro, I tried, but her reply was, "I know he's there because I just saw him walk across the street and if you value your relationship, you will put him on the phone." I said to my friend who quickly told me that he wanted to, but the voice in the phone was getting aggressive and threatening to end his relationship just like what mine was about to experience. "What?" I was surprised to now learn that the whispering voice truly wanted to end my relationship with Angela. Now the truth about their intention was out there and I was determined to fight that. The only problem was that even if I was determined, I wasn't the only one in the equation, and the conundrum in all this was to keep Angela on my side all the time – only that I had my own annoying habits that she would be required to love to see from time to time.

Anyway, even if she had tried to flip the numbers, the lunch with Kris happened and many other encounters followed. That was just my way of life and trying to stop that was very difficult, even by my own efforts. The day at my friend's place drove me back to living a cautious life. Even if I wanted to ignore this whole stalking thing, it was clear that it grew to unprecedented levels by each week, and I just could not afford to stay relaxed. And, since the lunch with Kris, I found myself wandering back to my old ways – cheating and more cheating was to follow.

However, I could feel that, this time, I was a little bit cautious. With me back in the 'game' as we used to call it, I had to always be watchful who watches me. But because the stalkers were always on my tail, there were many times that Angela would question my behavior. We would fight, become distant for a day or two locked in separate worlds only to fix things later. I can't lie to say that I enjoyed life or arguing with Angela that was always draining and even scary because I couldn't shake the feeling that she could just get up and leave me forever in the middle of one of the arguments. With that being said, I guess you might be wondering why then did I keep on cheating on her when I was scared of her leaving me – especially when there was someone giving her information about my dealings willingly. My response to that is, maybe I enjoyed clubbing and women more than I enjoyed being at home. Therefore, even though I feared the worst with Angela could happen, I just, sometimes, thought the trade-off would be worth it. Crazy, right?

Angela would visit with my family from time to time and spend a weekend there. Sometimes I would feel bad and remain home when she was away, but sometimes I would just up the tempo in terms of all my shenanigans. And don't think she wouldn't come back and know – she would know everything because the stalkers would have packaged all the details nicely for her. I just had ceased to mind that, as long as we talked through things and understood each other. One thing that I was now in the habit of saying was that I never slept with any of the girls. Angela would, sometimes, believe me because that's just what I do, I found a way out of every story.

So, this weekend, she left our home and decided to visit with my parents. She took both our children, and explained to me, she was going to be returning on Sunday. Left alone for the weekend, I immediately decided to take a chance while my family was hours away. I knew that even if I went out and came back early in the morning, she would never know about this because the drive from where they were was hours away. I was free to do whatever I wanted. I knew that the stalkers would be lurking, but I just didn't mind them at all. This time, I thought I was going to dodge them, somehow.

Soon after making that decision, I found myself and friends driving to this fully packed beach. There were all sorts of girls around and the place looked like it was full of life, so who was I not to get into the mood of this place? I decided I should just 'catch on' to the fun and just ride along with the rest of the people that were there, including my outgoing friends. However, I was, all the time, worried of being followed or seen by the 'wandering' eye. So I stayed cautious of where I was and who was around me all the time, even though I knew that my stalker would not just reveal themselves besides lurking in the shadows.

As I fell into temptations with my friends, we came across an interesting group of girls who had parked their cars close to ours, I remained cautious and never wanted to stay in open areas where I could be exposed by the distant eye. You could be wondering why go into all this trouble just for the company of some new and random ladies – but this was our way of life with my friends. It's like we used that as oxygen – it gave us a reason to be alive. Funny as it sounds, we seemed to enjoy doing this over and over again.

So as soon as we saw these girls, there were no two ways about it other than hoping out of our vehicle and letting our presence known. We always did it in a very special way that made it difficult for anyone to resist the kind of charm we let out. We had been in the game for a long time and we knew which buttons to press. It was as easy as that! The girls expectedly became entertained and agreed to share their time with us as we quickly chose who to pick among ourselves. You know when guys meet girls, each of the guys should pick their own girl – and the girls know this, so they will be ready for those kinds of things.

In the end, we combined our parties and partied together for as long as we could. We popped bottles and danced to some generous tunes from the radio. It made me forget about all my problems as expected, I let my guard down, paved the way for the stalkers to see as they wanted too. When the time was getting late, the girls said they wanted to go, but we did not want to lose such a wonderful company so early. We just could not let the evening end prematurely like that. So we sent out invitations for them to join our nightly gathering. The girls agreed and they made some phone calls, I think they were telling whoever was back at their homes that they had found some cool guys to spend the rest of the evening with.

From the time we left the beach to a more private place, we had the time of our lives. We did many things with the girls and the ecstasy that I missed from back in the day was back! At the moment, I could care less who was watching me. I met this girl and she knew how to press all my buttons, we exchanged numbers and promised to get into a replay of this wonderful moment that we both enjoyed. Seeing me like this made my friends really happy about me. I wasn't that paranoid guy always looking around and behaving like I would point a gun at anyone that passed by me.

As the old adage says, whatever goes up shall come down, indeed, we pulled down the curtains on this highly entertaining night we had with the girls from the beach. I went back to an empty home with one of the girls with the possibility of being caught in the act. Nonetheless, I was highly under the influence without a care in my body. It's something about temptation that gets me every time, even when I have everything to lose. I woke up early the next morning to make sure the apartment was straightened up to how it was before Angela left. One thing I know about women is that they are very observant when it comes to their territory.

With Angela returning home from my parents, I tried to look excited about seeing her and cracked some jokes as I greeted my family.

But in all honesty, I felt guilt caused by my action giving my time to another woman in our home. But I was surprised to see all my jokes just going to waste as Angela kept on staring at me as she unpacks. Can she see the guilt written all over my face or does she see something that has been left out of place? A day past as I returned home from work Angela suddenly tossed a pile of letters before me and said she found them stacked in her underwear drawer. I opened them and found them narrating every move that I made during this past weekend, including what transpired when I went for a private celebration with my weekend friends.

Oh, and by the way, I was told to ask you who the volleyball girl was as she handed me a bracelet. There was no easy way to deny all of this like I was used to doing. My only chance was to stick to facts that no solid proof was presented and letters from a person who would say whatever to ruin our relationship. Worked like a charm or is Angela allowing me to think she's naive?

But this was extreme! I could hear Angela as she was speaking, but my main focus was on this person entering my home where my kids sleep and all this is because of me. I found myself wondering how they got in so I began to search for unlocked windows. Stepping into our bedroom to find one window unlatched and the screen to the window had been taken off and placed on the ground below. Not only was I extremely upset about the possibilities of the stalker entering my home, but I found myself questioning Angela if she set all this up herself. I had a very hard time getting past the fact that just so happens the weekend she was away a window was left unlatched.

According to the stalkers, their latest stunt of placing letters and the bracelet in the underwear drawer of my last accused encounter was meant to be the final straw to my relationship. They thought that this time, my relationship was just going to go off the rails and leave everything falling apart. I feared for the same thing to happen, but somehow, I was very fortunate to live another day without having to count myself as someone who just got dumped by the mother of his children. But even as I think that I had gotten away with it, it left an indelible mark in the heart of Angela.

For the next two days, I could see the amount of pain in her eyes. I tried to stay at home so that she sees that I was still committed to our relationship, but that was all effort I did in vain. The worst part about all my actions was that, I'm pretty sure it ate into her confidence levels. I most likely drove her into doubting herself and she may have started to doubt her ability to be a partner that was capable of being loved by anyone - perhaps that was the reason why she hung on to me even when I cheated on her on countless occasions. Thinking about that really drove me to a significant amount of pain – something I did not usually do for her.

A few days passed and we began laughing together once again. As this happened, it was all in the eyes of our stalker. Imagine, they thought we were going to break up, but were surprised to see that we were actually laughing and making all sorts of jokes with the kids. I even started to spend more time at home to show that home was where I really wanted to be. This should really have pissed off the stalker because what followed from her was kind of drastic!

One beautiful morning, I decided to step outside for some fresh air and come back to talk to the family about the plans for the rest of the day. I was surprised to be greeted by a strangely poised car of ours in the driveway. What? I immediately took my eyes to the wheels and discovered that all of them had been slashed using a knife. Strange!

I knew that it was them and now they were really getting me scared. I sat down near the car and once again started thinking what I could have done to make this person hate me this much? I could not find the answers to all these questions. After a while when I had gone back to tell Angela about the bad news, I then realized that it was the stalker who was getting angry because of my growing connection with Angela when they had thought that they put the final nail to our relationship.

Vibrations enter my phone, incoming private caller. "Hello." I bet you think you're the man huh? I bet you think, just because you are able to manipulate your dumb baby mama into staying with you, she doesn't have a motion set in play of her own huh? "Whatever!" Do you really believe she is allowing you to be the only one to enjoy himself? Who cares, why are you calling me? We just thought you should know, your baby mama has been enjoying the company of another man and by the way, congratulations on your new born baby, "she may not be yours." Silence followed by a dial tone.

The stalker will say anything to break me, I thought to myself. Trying to convince myself not to let them get to me. But the problem was, when have they ever been wrong when it came down to my relationship? Everything they have ever written about me in the letters given to Angela have been true! Shedding tears about Angela stepping out on me, I could handle, but the thought of my newborn baby girl possibly not being mine, ate me up inside from that day on. I cried out for God to make this go away. I refused to mention this phone call to anyone and chose to take this to my grave because regardless of these accusations to be true about Angela, I just knew I was the father of our newborn baby girl.

For me, that was a very difficult phone call. Imagine them beginning to use my family to get to me. I needed to do something about it, but the question was always how was I going to be able to do so, if I didn't know where to start, nor did I know surely who was behind it.

"No better opportunity to come up with a brilliant plan while being on the road away from home". Brotha, I need your help. James replies, with a concern what's up? Brotha, I think my house is bugged somehow. James, huh? It has to be, there's no other way Lynn can know everything that I do. How else is she able to know everything that I do? I really don't know what's going on right now, but it has my mind all jacked up!" James replies, what do you mean? It's some crazy shit going on and I truthfully don't know who's behind it. James replies, well talk to me, let's try to figure this out. Brotha, someone's playing games with me and they are taking it too far.

"How are the kids and Angela? They are fine, but I feel they may be in danger. You know, I try my best to keep my cool around Angela because I'm the man of the house and I can't allow myself to show any sign of weakness. But truth be told brotha, I'm afraid. I can't see how this person is so destined to hurt me, whomever they may be. I just know I need answers so I can connect these small pieces of a puzzle I am trying my best to complete. Will you help me? Because right now I feel like I am fighting a battle I cannot win. I got you bro, so what's the plan?

"First, I want you to know there have been some things that have taken place that has me questioning Angela." James drops his head. Bro, it may just be me, but when I got that phone call about you the other day, I promise you, that voice sounded like Angela or her sister. When he said that, I felt a cold breeze making its way through my veins. I immediately pulled over and parked by the roadside as I was so angry at this person.

James noticed that I was really angry and gave me a moment to calm down, so he did not say a word for a moment. The car hooter made some noise as I banged on the steering wheel while shouting all sorts of obscenities against the whispering voice. "I swear it better not be her!" I shouted while looking towards my friend now. And he responded kindly, "But we don't know for sure, maybe it's my girl taking my shenanigans out on you." He tried not to laugh as he said it. I knew he was trying to cheer me up, so I just smiled and shook my head as I headed back on the road.

"I just don't know how they are getting all this information about me, brotha. I think they may have bugged my home, I swear." "James yes, that's a possibility. I thought about getting some security company to come sweep my whole apartment, but I can't afford that shit." Anyways as I was thinking about it, I realized that even if I have my apartment swept for bugs, do you really believe it would slow the stalker down, I doubt it! The thought of me failing to bring the situation under control just had me all worked up while driving home.

"Bro, I see you're so stressed about his whole sweeping the house thing. But there has to be another way we can do this without having to pay a single cent." "Yes, indeed there is, because I got a plan. Are you listening?" As James listened to me talk, he discovered that I had come up with a brilliant idea. Getting out of work the next morning, James shows up to my apartment as planned. There's nothing like making up a story with hopes that the stalkers will take the bait. Brotha, I had this nice piece that came through to see me at my workplace, Oowee! James, stop lying? Brotha, I had her doing handstands and cartwheels by the end of the night, I got a new one on the team. We laughed to make it real. It's honestly all we spoke about that entire time.

When the time came for my friend to leave, he winked at me as he was exiting my door, hoping that we had set up a really strong trap for whoever was behind all that was happening with me at the time.

The following day, guess what? Apparently the stalker got the message. Because like clockwork, Angela approached me fussing about this made up story. I tell you, for the first time in about a year, I was relieved that I was finally right about something concerning the stalker. I stood in my own home questioning God if he was doing this to me. The weight of a ton was lifted off my chest because I believe he had turned his back on me. This battle I am facing is far from over, but I will not go down without a fight. I told Angela about my plan with James and thankfully she was quick to believe me.

Just like me, this whole thing that was taking place in our lives really scared Angela. Questions were now flying all over our heads. Are these listening devices also capable of taking videos? Could these people have been watching us naked in our home all the time? I felt hopeless while thinking about all this. All I could do was hope for things to get better as time passed.

The stalking continued as we also continued on with our lives. Even though it was difficult, we chose not to succumb to any pressure from these people because honestly, life still had to go on. I wasn't going to fall on a trap that I had no idea how long it was going to run. I simply did not know for sure how the stalker planned to play her script. I always refer to the stalker as 'her' because I was so sure at this moment that it was Lynn behind all this madness. And I was dying to see the day that this theory was going to be proved.

I actually did not know about all these confidence levels until I heard her talking to a certain lady that she invited to come over. I don't know how she knew her, but I could tell that they were talking about our issues as the lady kept on insisting that we both needed to be in the meeting in order to conjure up a solution faster. But she kept on insisting that she first wanted to say her mind alone, and she needed that lady to be honest with her if she should leave me. Hearing that drove a very cold breeze in my intestines. I held my stomach as I eavesdropped on them while pretending to be asleep in the bedroom.

So I was driving Angela into doubting herself? I made her feel like she's worth less than she was? Regardless of the ugliness of their conversation, I refused to take it to heart and I vowed while in bed that I was going to show her that she was worth more than she knew to me. In fact, I was always scared of losing her, but it's just that I was with the one with a problem of cheating and I was nowhere near her when it comes to being a great person to be in a relationship with.

As they were talking, the subject then changed to the exact reason why she had decided to invite that lady into our home – The recent actions that ended with new letters and a bracelet in her underwear drawer upon her return. While opening up the conversation, she started by saying that she believed me all the time when I explained to her that I never slept with those women, that we just had a few drinks together.

But the presence of these new letters and a bracelet brought so much doubt about anything else that I had said about my past actions. She now believed that I was sleeping with all the other girls that I had previously refused to have been sleeping with.

"So it seems that you don't believe your boyfriend's answers and explanations to your past conversations about these girls that he is always accused of being with by this stalker? And secondly, it looks like you don't accept that you're wrong as he wanted you to believe all along or make things up in your head. The final thing is that you now have proof of a bracelet that was purposely left behind by another woman?" I raised my head from the pillow when she said those things. Indeed, I had accused my girl before of making things up and she believed me, but now there was evidence right in front of her. I did not know what to do at that point.

Angela responded to this lady and said all her trust in me was gone. She said that she used to think that she was giving me a benefit of the doubt before but she was just being stupid. Really? That really did not sit well with me. I vowed that I was going to do things better from now.

Indeed, when the lady left, I pretended as if I did not hear a single word of their conversation, but when I saw her, I saw an opportunity to make things right by starting to ask for forgiveness about the past weekend. I vowed that from now on, I was going to try to be better. I knew that it sounded like a broken record for then, but it had to be said so that I follow it up with action. I reminded her of all the good things she had done for me and the kids, and really showed her that she is the sanest person in our house, something that kind of cheered her up. My words were followed by actions as I, for the first time in a long time, cooked for her and cleaned the house as she sat and watched the tv.

A few days passed and we began laughing together once again. As this happened, it was all in the eyes of our stalker. Imagine, they thought we were going to break up, but were surprised to see that we were actually laughing and making all sorts of jokes with the kids. Now imagine, me waking up from this dream I was having, and returning back to reality.

In the long efforts of trying to keep something together, there is always a possibility of losing. I, too, happened to have lost the plot at some point as I kept on telling Angela that I was this close to solving this while conundrum. Whether I was right, or not, I did not know. But what I knew was that the stalker was out to make sure that my relationship with Angela ended, and must be in a way that was going to leave me in pain. Knowing me, I was going to be left in pain if the relationship ended NOT in my terms. If it was going to be in my terms, I could stomach that and move on with my life like there was nothing happening. Nevertheless, with Angela there were kids involved and that drove me to thinking of mending things with her no matter the cost.

Stage 2

The new introduction of Lynn into the story really got me thinking a lot. Changing where I lived and deciding to move my family from their known location to somewhere else. Moving three floors up so that it would not be an easy access to our home. Installing cameras facing in every direction with hopes of catching the stalker. Lynn! I breathed heavily as I thought about her. This had to come to an end. I wanted my life back. I just could not carry on like this any longer.

However, I soon discovered something that was really shocking to me. I found out that Lynn was a good friend of one of my best friends' girlfriends' friend, but outside my circle of friends. I didn't know what to make of this, so I probed those further, asking questions of her whereabouts. Why didn't anyone alert me of this till now, is it possible this friend could be relaying information about me? Now my mind is once again triggered, racing, in search for answers. There was no question that my friend had no clue Lynn was a friend of his girlfriend's best friend. Truthfully, if Lynn walked by him today he probably wouldn't recognize her.

So, eventually, I found out through the girlfriend of James that Lynn was living in the same apartments, the same building as I was. Yes, you heard me! We shared the same gate and so forth, but I never knew about her presence. Now, the big question that kept on ringing in my mind was, "With everything she put me through, she must be insane to show no fear of being my next door neighbor.

The fact that I found out Lynn so happened to be living in the same apartment complex as us really drove me crazy. I was puzzled at this moment. What are the odds of moving closer to the person that you assume is your stalker, and to be placed in the same building as them? Being harassed on the phone every night by someone I assumed was the whispering voice that lived just around the corner was something that had me scrambling to maintain full control of my emotions. But the worst part was that even with all these meaningful theories building in my mind, there was no way I was just going to get up and accuse her without evidence. So in other words, I was still stuck between a hard place and a rock concerning the stalker.

To be honest, I was left so confused about all this new information. I wanted to believe with all my heart that it was not her, but how could she not be? I was convinced it was her, it had to be her! I could not wait to face her and ask some difficult questions. I wanted to know why she was doing this to me. But then, I was held back because, as much as I was angry, I needed to lay my hands on concrete evidence first before going on an offensive against her.

However, on this day entering my newly secured apartment, Angela was explaining the arrival of new letters to me, she noticed our daughter slapping at the patio window because something had gotten her attention. She approached, moving the blinds apart to see what has gotten our daughters attention. It was then, when she noticed the 3rd tennis ball finding its way onto our patio. Sliding the patio door open, only to receive letters attached by rubber bands to each tennis ball.

Listening to Angela trying to explain this to me in first thought was, bullshit! So you're telling me someone was accurate enough to throw tennis balls three floors up, landing perfectly onto our patio? What is a man in my position supposed to believe? Of course I wanted to believe her with all my heart, but it was episodes like this that made it very difficult not to question her. To top it off, after checking the camera footage, no human form was present. Regardless, of the fact I had a very difficult time believing Angela's story, I hung on to the hope of the possibility that the stalkers were capable.

Even though I questioned her, I chose to trust her because I thought it was just the paranoia playing in my head. You reckon that the same paranoia had me suspecting my friends of being behind this, yet they were the ones that were always by my side as I went through this ugly period of my life. So I chose to stick to Angela and gave her my trust.

At this point, we needed help really fast, but like people in shock, we never thought of getting someone to help us or alert the authorities because the evidence was plenty – from the letters being placed on our door for Angela to find, to the calls that were being made to me. We soon realized we were dealing with people that went to extreme measures to make our lives a living hell. So, I decided to go report to the police, but there was a problem. It's not so easy requesting a restraining order with no name to give.

There was nothing the police could do using such evidence. When this fell through, I decided to take the law into my own hands by purchasing a gun to ensure safety for my family. Trying to stay focused at work with a twisted mind, only to be alarmed by a recurring phone call as predicted. What now, unable to hide my frustration as the sound of laughter and whispers enter my ear. Minutes later, I heard a familiar chiming in the background, I felt my stomach turn as my phone went to complete silence followed by a dial tone.

Dialing Angela to confront her as the stalker, "So all this time it was you?" I shouted with much conviction. But Angela acted confused, as if she was coming out of a deep sleep and had no idea about me being called by anyone. I wasn't convinced at all. So I lashed out as she could hear the frustration being pushed onto her about hearing our home clock in the background when the stalker called. Still, denying she had nothing to do with the phone call I had received. Therefore, I could only assume that Angela was being truthful.

A week later, Angela found out that a friend of hers had the exact same clock in her home and brought this to my attention. But even if she did, I acted as if she was the one that was trying to cover her tracks. There was no need trying to convince me that a friend had an identical clock in her home where I have never been, that chimed in the background causing her to silence her phone followed by ending the call.

I was enraged, and I tried by all means to fix things for the sake of our kids. Now with a gun, I left work one day feeling like a stone cold killer, because of threats of harming my children. And my suspicions had been lifted off Angela and back to Lynn. Now I wanted to finish her off, including her accomplices if they lived with her. So soon after coming home, I went straight to the closet and got hold of my gun. Angela tried to stop me to no avail, and the next thing is I found myself banging on Lynn's door.

Breathing heavy as tears flowed down my face. Continuously banging on her door as my anxiety played a major role causing me to take a seat on some nearby steps. Suddenly glancing up to the sound of Angela's voice screaming no! Noticing in her arms are my two precious daughters relieving me of my rage. I hit my head with the bottom of my handgun as I cried out loud and returned to my apartment. She could live for another day, but the message had been sent, so I thought!

I decided it was time to make a change, so I moved my family away from the city I once loved. Welcoming us into their home my parents were a great sight to see, hours away in Greenleaf, TX. Finally, I was able to breathe in life miles away from a nightmare that almost ruined my family. Nonetheless, the nightmare was far from over. Strange events followed him into his parents' home. Frustrations of not being able to escape the stalker, eventually led to the stalker getting what she wanted as Angela and I went our separate ways.

I chose the single life rather than stepping up in being the man that Angela wanted me to be. I was at a breaking point in my life that I didn't know who to trust anymore. More so, because I believed deep down in my heart that Angela was the one responsible. I wouldn't allow myself to get past the fact, why I was never contacted by the stalker while she was around? Why did she have to disguise her voice with a soft whisper? I couldn't get past the fact, why did Angela only receive letters when I wasn't around? At this moment, I was ready to lose it all and go back to being alone.

Nevertheless, I still felt like I was the one behaving like a fool when I was supposed to be doing right by my family. It was difficult for Angela to finally take her belongings and leave me. When she and the kids left, a part of me left with them, I felt lonely. I felt like I needed something to hold me together and what she and I were experiencing wasn't it. It was only pushing me further away.

A few days after she was gone, I started to miss her and the kids. I realized that I was having a difficult time when it comes to moving on. When she was around, I always thought that it was so easy to replace her whenever we separated, but I was very wrong to think like that. In these moments, I still felt the presence of the stalker still existed. These feelings were soon to be elevated to something real when the calls started all over again. I was very worried when they started because I was like, this is now going to be my whole life. I will be living life having to watch over my shoulders. I questioned the stalkers why they would still call me when they got what they wanted because Angela and I have separated.

As I asked, they would laugh and say they know that she's gone, but now it was time for them to mess with my head. Indeed, they were messing with my head in ways I couldn't even start to imagine. I was sacred for things like my job and so forth. I then realized this person was not only out to mess with my head, but to actually destroy my life completely. These are the kinds of things to expect from a very bitter ex-girlfriend alone - My thoughts went back to Lynn. By now, I was very confused because I had thought if I had given the stalker exactly what she wanted, why is she still contacting me?

Months of loneliness on top of missing my kids, I picked up my phone to call Angela. Some may question why I would reach out to Angela in working things out when I believed her to be my stalker. But, when you love something so desperately you will find a way to make things right. Angela and I slowly started to work on our relationship after that day. When she came back home, we were doing this 'for the sake of our children.' For sure, we believed that was the biggest reason for now and everything else was going to be worked on with time. Reuniting our family was the greatest feeling for the both of us. Right now, I was a humbled man. The stalking had really put me in a place where I was shown that, after all, I wasn't that guy I wanted to portray out there.

Knowing everything Angela had gone through, I was content on showing her that she was highly appreciated. Like I said, the trust between us was severely damaged and needed some real work if it was ever to get mended. As such, Angela would not let me in. She was constantly reminding me if I was sure she was what I wanted, and that alone became a frustration. I hated it when someone kept on asking me the same question over and over again! Therefore, as time went on, I became distant once again, and Angela noticed the change. As that happened, she also took a dramatic change in how she handled herself in our home. One night, I was alarmed in my sleep, hearing voices as Angela paced around our home.

With everything that took place in our relationship, it was very possible my mind was starting to play tricks on me. Sometimes I couldn't sleep, fearing that one day Angela would appear with a knife and stab me to death because of all the pain I had put her through. But I wasn't ready to die so I spent some of my nights half asleep, just watching her. I struggled to understand how she accepted my actions – at least to the point of not leaving me forever. I know, I could have been just acting out of fear, but for me, that was necessary fear, I had to experience it and tread with caution even in my own home.

Final Chapter

Years after the whole drama with the stalker, I wanted to get my life back on track, and the first thing I did was to connect with Angela and try to fix things with her. But by me saying that, it doesn't mean it was an easy road to travel, I had many mistakes that I made regardless of the things I had been going through in my life. Me in clear view of Angela's pain hurt me to the point I could no longer see her this way, even if it meant I had to walk away. As I went on about my life, I met a new girl, and her name was Taylor. I don't know how things happened, but it started like we wanted a night together, but we clicked and it matured into a relationship.

She knew about Angela, but I did not want Angela to know about her, so she was a very closely guarded secret. Speaking of secrets, I also did not want Taylor to find out about my past, especially with the drama caused by the stalker, who, by the way, was still present in my life, making calls to me as she wanted. Even when she still called, the frequency was now low and I never had nasty incidents like the slashing of my car tires. So all in all, I could say that the situation had greatly improved!

My life right now, at this moment, felt like it was becoming normal again. I honestly loved it until the day when the stalker decided to call Taylor. She received what she thought was a routine phone call from a client requesting a hair appointment, but no, she was being called to be told about all my past behaviors. When she told me about this later, I knew that problems were about to start over again. The feeling just left me puzzled with nothing much I felt I could do about it. I felt hopeless and powerless. Taylor thought the call was just from a concerned citizen warning her about my past, but she did not know it could have been my stalker now calling her. That, I chose to make it a secret that she was never going to find out because I knew that if she did, she wouldn't want to be involved with someone with such a messed up life.

But my plan to keep this a secret backfired badly because the stalker increased the calls to Taylor, making sure they got my attention through her. It got to a point where I could clearly see that things are now at hectic levels. At some point, I thought it's now causing me to act selfish because if I cared about Taylor, I should have told her as soon as the calls started that I had a stalker that caused havoc in my life – just to give her a fair warning. But I did not see any reason to do all that.

After that, I watched my phone ring for days as the stalker also started increasing her calls to me. Sometimes it rang while I was with Taylor, and she could see that things were not all ok with me. But when she asked, I would always tell her that it was alright.

After a few days, Angela called notifying me of some mail that was addressed to me from the Attorney General that she had received. I was very surprised to hear her ask about another child that I had with another woman. I tried to convince Angela I was unaware of another child, which I clearly knew about the possibility, because it was my secret. I was devastated because my secret I wanted to keep was coming out. Sad, I now lived my life knowing there is no secret that would remain because of this unknown person, who could even be Angela.

This unknown person was calling Taylor with the aim of destroying my relationship with her. Now it was time for me to out think the stalker. Approaching Taylor with this information brought to my attention by Angela was very difficult for me to do, but I had no choice. I felt Taylor would be more understanding if it came from me, rather than the unknown person. Approaching Taylor in fear of losing her, I had no choice but to tell her the disappointing news.

A few days after the disappointing news to Taylor, returning home from work she approaches me with the word of being contacted by the unknown person.

Over the years myself and Angela have grown into mature amazing co-parents. Putting our children first and overcoming all obstacles. But, till this day, I am unaware of the unknown person.

I started telling my story in search of finding closure, but instead I felt disgusted with everything my eyes could see written by my own hands. I now understand reasoning for everything that was brought onto me and why whomever chose to do it. I have been angry for many years, but now I am grateful enough to say, I am truly sorry!

Made in the USA
Columbia, SC
28 May 2021

38597879R00050